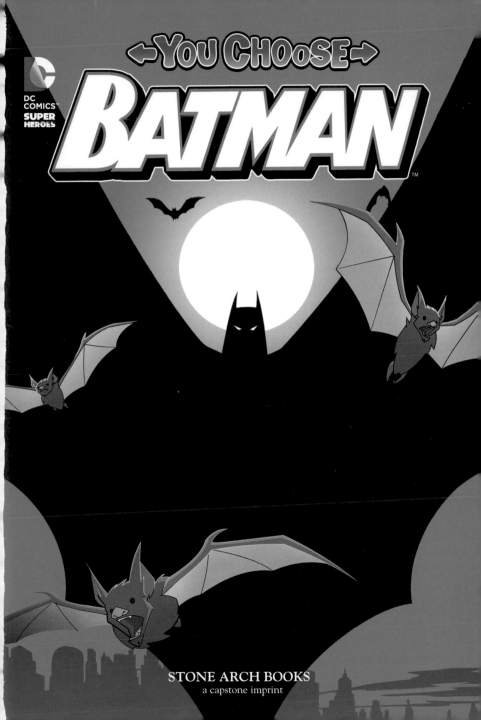

You Choose Stories: Batman
is published by Stone Arch Books,
A Capstone Imprint
1710 Roe Crest Drive
North Mankato, Minnesota 56003
www.capstonepub.com

Cataloging-in-Publication Data is available
on the Library of Congress website.
ISBN: 978-1-4342-9708-2 (library binding)
ISBN: 978-1-4342-9712-9 (paperback)
ISBN: 978-1-4965-0212-4 (eBook)

Summary: Mr. Freeze blankets Gotham City in a blizzard,
turning the city into an enormous snow globe. With your
help, Batman will melt the super-villain's Summer Freeze!

Printed in Canada.
092014   008478FRS15

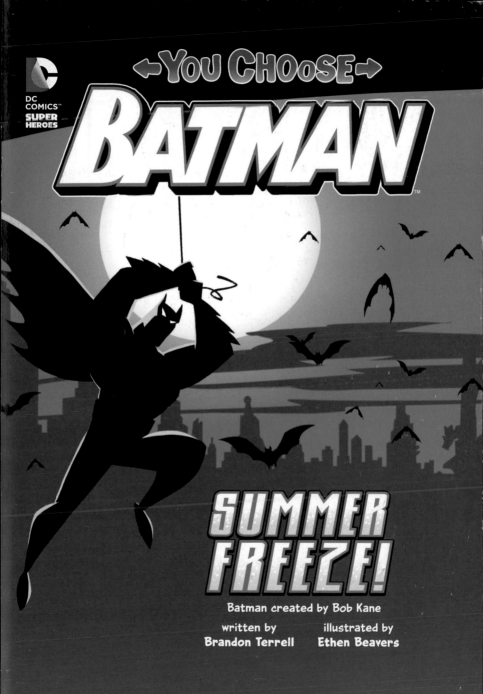

DC COMICS™
SUPER HEROES

←YOU CHOOSE→

BATMAN™

SUMMER FREEZE!

Batman created by Bob Kane

written by
Brandon Terrell

illustrated by
Ethen Beavers

Mr. Freeze has blanketed Gotham City in a blizzard, turning the city into an enormous snow globe. Only YOU can help the Dark Knight melt the super-villain's Summer Freeze!

Follow the directions at the bottom of each page. The choices YOU make will change the outcome of the story. After you finish one path, go back and read the others for more Batman adventures!

"Freeze! Stay where you are!"

The jewelry store security guard rushes out onto the sidewalk, hot on the heels of the thief.

The robber wears a black mask to hide his face and carries a duffel bag filled with cash and jewelry. He laughs. "Not a chance!"

He ducks down a dark alleyway.

Gotham City is in the middle of a record heat wave, with no relief in sight. Even now, at this late-night hour, the temperature is sweltering. Because of the maddening heat, Gotham City's crime rate has risen like the mercury in a thermometer.

Turn the page.

The thief dashes down the alley, completely unaware that Batman, the Dark Knight, is watching him from atop a nearby building.

Batman drops into the alley, landing in front of the jewelry store robber. The thief cries out in wide-eyed panic. "Here! Just take it!" He thrusts his duffel bag into Batman's chest and dashes back the way he came.

"I prefer gadgets over jewelry," Batman says. He flings a Batarang at the fleeing robber. The thief trips and hits the pavement hard.

The Bat-Signal suddenly shines bright in the sky, and the radio in Batman's cowl — tuned to Gotham City Police Department's frequency — bursts to life.

"*Skrrzz* — All units, report to Gotham Harbor," it says. "A cargo ship has crashed into the piers. Reports say the ship is . . . *skrzz* . . . made entirely out of ice."

Ice? There's only one villain who'd possibly captain a ship like that, Batman thinks. *Mr. Freeze.*

The Dark Knight returns the bag of money and jewelry to its rightful owner. Then he drops off the bound thief at the doorstep of the Gotham City Police Department.

When he arrives at Gotham Harbor, Batman sees the enormous ship carved of ice. It has crashed into the docks, splintering wood in its wake. A few harbor patrol officers have been encased in blocks of ice near a run-down warehouse. Others work hard to free them.

Police cars surround the harbor, their lights flickering and bouncing off buildings. Batman spies Police Commissioner James Gordon and Detective Harvey Bullock and approaches them.

"Have you found anything?" Batman asks.

"You mean aside from the giant floating ice sculpture and the cop-sicles?" answers Detective Bullock.

Gordon ignores his snide comment. "Clues? Nothing yet." He wipes his sweaty brow with a handkerchief.

Turn the page.

Batman and Gordon examine the ship from a safe distance. As they do, blue light explodes above the skyline. The earth shakes. The air crackles.

Then the light vanishes, but something far worse appears in its place. Blue, crystalline ice expands over Gotham City. It stretches toward the horizon in each direction.

The temperature plummets, and snowflakes begin falling from the sky.

"What is that?" a stunned Gordon asks.

"A dome made of ice," Batman replies. "And it's covering the whole city."

Batman's breath plumes in front of his face. Police officers panic. Commissioner Gordon barks orders into a walkie-talkie, demanding the airport cancel flights and reroute circling airplanes.

Turn to page 12.

There is a sudden burst of static from his walkie. Then the voice of Victor Fries — aka Mr. Freeze — says, "Good evening, Commissioner. Batman. Quite the weather we're having, isn't it? This is merely a taste of my power. While I am in control, Gotham City will be blanketed in this bitter chill like a snow globe."

Batman must find Mr. Freeze before the whole city is permanently buried in snow. The harbor must hold some clue as to the villain's whereabouts.

But where will the Caped Crusader begin his search?

If Batman searches the ice ship, turn to page 13.
If Batman searches the warehouse, turn to page 37.

"Have your men inspect the warehouse," Batman tells Commissioner Gordon. "I'm going to board the ship and look for clues."

Cautiously, Batman steps onto the ship's deck. The traction on his boots makes it easy to walk on the slick surface. He examines the top deck, including the bridge.

Nothing.

Steps lead down to the ship's cargo hold. Batman descends below deck. Through the ice at his feet, he can see the deep blue water of Gotham Bay.

As he enters the ship's hold, Batman hears a crunch underfoot. He has triggered a booby trap. A slab of ice crashes behind him, blocking the steps. The walls rumble and begin to close in on him. If Batman does not act quickly, he'll be flattened for sure!

If Batman uses his laser to cut a hole in the floor, turn to page 41.

If Batman uses a small bomb to blast one wall, turn to page 51.

Batman knows Gotham City's underground labyrinth well. There is a sewer entrance nearby that leads directly into the museum, near the boiler room.

The Dark Knight climbs down into the the city's sewers. There is a little heat left trapped beneath the city, and the tunnels are surprisingly warm.

Batman runs through them, using the night-vision goggles in his cowl to see. Rats squeak and scurry out of his way.

Sure enough, the tunnels lead him directly under the museum's boiler room. He climbs a ladder, removes the floor grate, and begins to pull himself up.

It is then that he hears voices outside the room.

Mr. Freeze's men!

"The boss wants us to use this grenade — he calls it a Freeze Pop — on the boiler," the voice outside the door says.

Then the door swings open, and two of Mr. Freeze's men enter.

Batman has little time to react. He leaps from the floor grate as the henchmen see him.

"Hey!" shouts the first man in the door. He is holding a blue canister in his hands. Surprised by the Caped Crusader's presence, he drops the can. "Oh no! The Freeze Pop!"

KA-BOOM!

The room explodes in a bright blue flash.

Batman cannot move.

When his sight returns, he finds the whole room is covered in ice and frost. He's frozen to the floor, rooted in place by the henchman's appropriately named Freeze Pop. His instincts led him to cover his face with his cape. He was right to do so. It is the only part of him not blanketed in ice.

There's no way out, though. Not until the ice thaws, or the Gotham City Police Department comes to his rescue.

Turn the page.

By then, Mr. Freeze will be long gone.

Batman can only hope the super-villain releases Gotham City from his deadly dome before he makes his escape.

THE END

To follow another path, turn to page 12.

Afraid that the polar bears would easily escape the projectile net, Batman searches his belt for another gadget. He finds a small black capsule, throws it in front of the advancing bears, and covers his head with his cape.

FWASH!

Brilliant white light flashes through the room. Notchka and Shaka bellow in anger as they stumble blindly about. One of them snaps its jaws in Batman's general direction, but the Caped Crusader easily escapes to safety.

He hides behind the exhibit's massive glacier model until the bears thrash their way out of the Arctic hall and back into the museum.

When the bears have disappeared, Batman slinks cautiously back into the museum. He hears the two animals thundering down the hall, heading toward the museum's storeroom.

Batman follows.

The storeroom is a long, cavernous warehouse at the rear of the museum.

Turn the page.

The storeroom holds the remainder of the museum's priceless artifacts. There are rows and rows stacked high with crates. Scattered floodlights hang from the ceiling, giving off pockets of light. The remainder of the massive room is draped in blackness.

Ahead of Batman, the two polar bears run out an open metal delivery door on the far side of the room.

Mr. Freeze cannot be far away.

Batman discovers a broken wooden crate. Stenciled on it are two words: ARKHAM EXHIBIT. The museum was collecting artifacts from Gotham's infamous asylum and its occupants for a special exhibit.

Freeze must have found another one of his suits among the collection, Batman thinks.

As he dashes for the delivery door, Batman hears the roar of many engines outside in the blizzard. Mr. Freeze and his goons are driving away on what appear to be snowmobiles.

Notchka and Shaka run beside the villain, who is indeed wearing a new robotic suit and is driving the lead machine.

Batman's hand goes to his Utility Belt.

The Batmobile could easily intercept the fleeing Mr. Freeze. But the rear henchman — who revs his snowmobile's engine and begins to skitter across the snowfall — is close, too.

If Batman follows in the Batmobile, turn to page 66.
If Batman tries to steal the snowmobile, turn to page 82.

There's not much time. Batman skids to a stop and presses a button on his Utility Belt.

Soon after, headlights pierce the wintry haze, and the Batmobile rumbles through the snow, braking mere feet from the Caped Crusader.

Batman leaps into the car, grips the wheel, and stomps on the accelerator.

VROOOOOM!

The ice cream truck has a good lead now. Batman can barely make out the vehicle's shape through the falling snow. He does his best to be careful on the slick roads. One false move, and he'll lose the truck for good.

The freak blizzard has struck Gotham City unprepared, and many motorists have either stranded their cars or found themselves stuck in traffic. Batman weaves around them carefully, but the ice cream truck has no problem driving up on sidewalks, narrowly missing frigid pedestrians wearing T-shirts and flip-flops.

Batman cruises through an intersection.

Drawing close to the truck, a hatch on top swings open and one of Freeze's henchmen appears. In his hands is what appears to be a blue bazooka.

"This can't be good," Batman mutters.

BA-BOOOM!

A large ball of ice erupts from the bazooka, striking the Batmobile's hood and denting the sleek car.

Turn to page 23.

Batman swerves as a second ice ball is fired at the Batmobile. This shot narrowly misses, striking a street lamp instead. The back tires of the Batmobile lose traction, and the Dark Knight must fight to keep control of the vehicle.

Ahead, the ice cream truck turns left. It skids through the intersection, its tail smashing into the side of a parked car before driving off.

Batman slows and navigates carefully around the turn.

As he does, a large chunk of ultra-strong ice from the bazooka strikes the Batmobile's windshield. The glass cracks, spreading out like a spiderweb. Following the ice cream truck has become dangerous, but Batman cannot afford to lose the henchmen's trail.

If Batman steers onto a different street, turn to page 54.
If Batman continues to follow the truck, turn to page 90.

Batman reaches for the net in the back of his Utility Belt. It looks like a long cylinder, but when thrown, it grows into a webbing of thick rope strong enough to hold the mightiest of villains.

The Caped Crusader quickly throws the net at the bears.

It expands, wrapping around both advancing polar bears and trapping them. They roar in anger. As they thrash about, Batman leaps onto the manmade glacier in the center of the exhibit.

Then the unthinkable happens. One of the bears' gnashing jaws bites down on the net. The thick rope snaps, and the creatures are free!

There is little time to react. The bears, furious at the pesky super hero, leap onto the glacier. The Caped Crusader searches his belt for another item to use, but it is too late.

One of the bears swipes at him with its massive paw. Batman is knocked back into a crevasse built in the glacier.

As he strikes the glacier wall, an avalanche of fake snow and ice fall down on him. The other bear uses its immense strength to split the glacier model in two and push it down in front of the crevasse, blocking Batman's escape.

Batman removes a communication device from his Utility Belt. He sends an urgent call to his partner, Robin. Until the Boy Wonder arrives, Batman will need to hold off the ferocious beasts with only his gloved hands.

There is no way he can stop Mr. Freeze now.

THE END

To follow another path, turn to page 12.

The remaining henchman fires his weapon.

Batman dives for the freeze gun, scooping it off the floor and squeezing the trigger. The two streams crash into one another, shattering in an explosion of ice crystals.

SKRAAASH!

Batman shields himself with his cape. Icicles pelt him like driving hail.

When the blast clears, the Caped Crusader is safe.

The henchman did not fare as well. He stands rooted in place like one of the wax figures. Icicles hang from his nose. His teeth chatter.

"Why don't you guys cool off for a bit?" Batman jokes.

The Caped Crusader races off to the museum's Ancient Egypt exhibit.

As Batman runs through the darkened museum, he notices the temperature inside has dropped significantly. His breath clouds, and he even spies snowflakes swirling from the ceiling.

Freeze's dome device is even affecting the museum, he thinks.

Ahead is the Ancient Egypt exhibit hall, including artifacts from Dr. Arvin Schimmell's excavation. Batman begins to hear a soft humming sound. Its volume increases the closer he gets.

The Dark Knight stops and begins to peer around the corner.

There is a sound behind him, a shuffle of feet.

One of Freeze's henchmen!

Batman turns to face the sound, but he is not fast enough.

THWACK!

Something heavy strikes the Dark Knight in the temple.

The world goes black.

The first thing Batman notices as he regains consciousness is the icy handcuffs around his wrists. He lies on an Egyptian sarcophagus.

Turn the page.

Around him are large models of the pyramids and the Sphinx. The walls have been painted in bright shades of red, orange, and yellow. Unlike the real desert, though, snow flutters from above and blankets the exhibit.

A handful of henchmen are positioned around the room. In the center of the exhibit, humming and emitting a blue glow, is a machine made of metal and tubes and glass. Its power is being drawn from the enormous Schimmell diamond within it.

The device that controls the dome, Batman concludes.

And standing next to it is Mr. Freeze.

Turn to page 30.

Mr. Freeze is an imposing villain. His robotic suit — topped with a transparent helmet that keeps his head at subzero temperatures — gives the villain amazing strength.

Mr. Freeze looks over and sees Batman is now awake.

"So nice of you to join us," he says. "I see you're admiring my latest invention." He gestures to the device. "A weapon strong enough to create a permanent force field made of ice around an entire city. My own wonderful snow globe to live inside. All powered by Dr. Schimmell's discovery.

"This is merely the tip of the iceberg," Mr. Freeze continues. "Now that the diamond is in my possession, I can create a dome wherever I go. And everyone inside its walls will feel as cold and trapped as I am."

Mr. Freeze has his back to the Caped Crusader. As the chilled villain speaks, Batman slips his fingers into his Utility Belt and removes his laser torch. He uses it on the handcuffs, silently freeing himself from his icy bonds.

There is a single Batarang left in his belt. If Batman can reach it, he'll have just one throw. He'd best make it count.

If Batman throws the Batarang at the dome device, turn to page 57.

If Batman throws the Batarang at Mr. Freeze, turn to page 68.

It is a long shot, but Batman's deductions are rarely wrong. He quickly types *FRIES* into the keypad.

The device's hum grows louder, more intense. Batman must cup his hands over his ears to block out the noise.

Something is wrong.

A blue light emanates from the device. It pulses once with a blinding light.

Batman is thrown back onto the cement, knocked unconscious.

He wakes to find Commissioner Gordon staring down at him.

"Batman, are you all right?" the commissioner asks.

Batman looks around. Sunlight floods the streets of Gotham City. The snow is melting. It drips from buildings and runs into the streets, making a slushy mess.

"Freeze's dome is gone," Batman says weakly. "It worked."

"I wish it were that simple," Gordon says. "Freeze is the one who spared us from the icy globe. Right before he fled Gotham City with the device and the Schimmell diamond."

If only the Dark Knight had tried one of the other possible passwords.

THE END

To follow another path, turn to page 12.

Before the henchmen reach his position, Batman silently climbs atop the nearest stack of crates. The henchmen hurry past, heading back to retrieve the device, unaware of the super hero's presence.

Mr. Freeze is alone with the snow globe. The Caped Crusader carefully steps from one crate to the next. He is at least ten feet in the air. When he reaches the villain's location, he leaps down into the light.

"Game over, Freeze," Batman says, landing expertly on the floor.

Mr. Freeze turns. He isn't fazed to see the Caped Crusader standing in front of him. He holds out the repaired snow globe. "I was told it still existed, but I didn't fully believe until just now," says the super-villain.

"It doesn't have to be like this," Batman says. "You still have some humanity, Victor. I know it."

"HAHAHA!" Mr. Freeze laughs, a cold sound that sends chills down Batman's spine.

The super-villain sets the snow globe safely aside on the crates.

"You will never stop me," he says.

"Never say never, Freeze," Batman answers.

Batman balls his hands into fists as Mr. Freeze attacks.

The villain's robotic suit makes him extremely strong. He lashes out with one arm. The Dark Knight reacts quickly. *FWOOSH!* Batman covers himself with his cape. The cape's ultra-strong fabric absorbs the mechanical blow.

Batman cannot hide for long. He reveals himself again, ready to fight. Mr. Freeze unleashes a flurry of punches. The Dark Knight blocks more than a dozen of them, but finally a punch sneaks through, connecting solidly with Batman's chest. *WHAM!*

The Dark Knight flies backward, crashing into another crate of Arkham artifacts.

SMAAAAASH!

The crate's contents spill to the floor.

Turn the page.

Amidst the foam packaging are two familiar items. One is a black and white umbrella, the kind used by the Penguin. The other is a large green mallet, a signature weapon of the Clown Prince of Crime, the Joker.

Mr. Freeze advances on the dazed hero. Batman must defend himself.

But with what?

If Batman uses the mallet, turn to page 60.
If Batman uses the umbrella, turn to page 78.

Before Batman investigates the ship, he decides to search the warehouse. The frozen guards outside mean a struggle took place. Maybe there will be a clue to Mr. Freeze's whereabouts hidden within.

The snow is coming down faster now, coating the ground with shimmering white and making it hard to see.

Batman enters the darkened warehouse. Large shipping containers are draped in shadow. A forklift is parked nearby.

Suddenly, the forklift roars to life! Its lights are blindingly bright, forcing Batman to shield his eyes with one arm. One of Mr. Freeze's henchmen drives the machine. Two others emerge from the shadows. In their hands are freeze guns identical to the weapon used by Mr. Freeze.

Batman has been ambushed!

Turn to page 39.

Batman dives to one side as the forklift barrels past. He rolls into a crouch and throws a Batarang at one of the henchmen. It strikes the thug's freeze gun.

The second henchman fires a blast of ice that whooshes past Batman's head and hits the container behind him, instantly freezing the metal. Before he can shoot again, Batman pounces on him.

"Police! Put your hands up!" Two officers stand in the warehouse entrance, weapons drawn.

"Wait!" Batman shouts. It is too late. The third henchman fires at the officers. The icy beam strikes their legs, and their weapons clatter to the cement.

Batman rushes to their aid. Meanwhile, the dazed henchmen flee out the warehouse's back door.

Batman checks the frozen officers. "Are you hurt?" he asks.

Turn the page.

"We're fine," one grumbles, struggling to break free.

"Stop those punks," says the other, pointing at the warehouse's open rear entrance.

Batman follows the goons into the driving snow. The henchmen are Batman's best shot at finding Mr. Freeze's whereabouts.

Outside, an ice cream truck is skidding to a stop. Its back cargo door flings open, and the three henchmen leap aboard.

The truck driver revs the engine. Its back tires spew ice and slush. It fishtails back and forth before gaining traction and roaring away.

Batman knows that if he does not act quickly, he'll lose the henchmen.

If Batman follows in the Batmobile, turn to page 20.
If Batman fires his grapnel gun at the truck, turn to page 100.

Batman hopes the laser in his Utility Belt will be strong enough to cut through the ice. He kneels down and aims the laser's red beam at the floor. It works!

ZZZRT!

The laser carves a circle wide enough for Batman to escape.

The Dark Knight takes a deep breath and holds it as he kicks free the circle of ice.

Freezing water rushes into the hold. Even through his Batsuit, the Dark Knight feels its numbing claws. He waits until the hold is flooded, then dives for the hole in the floor and swims to safety.

Batman kicks for the water's surface. His lungs burn. Spots swirl in his vision.

Finally he reaches the surface, feels the cool air, and gasps for breath.

"There! In the water!" Commissioner Gordon calls out. Searchlights scour the water as Batman swims toward the docks.

Turn the page.

Two police officers assist in pulling Batman from Gotham Bay. Once on land again, the Caped Crusader shudders. He's still gripped by the water's icy chill. The thick, fat snowflakes swirling around him do not help.

"Some of Mr. Freeze's goons were holed up in the warehouse," Gordon tells him. "Unfortunately, they got away."

"Too bad," Batman says. It takes all his strength to keep his teeth from chattering. "They could have led us straight to Mr. Freeze."

***

Once at the Batcave, the Caped Crusader's alter ego, billionaire Bruce Wayne, changes into dry clothes. He sits in front of the cave's high-tech computers, thinking about his next move.

Behind him, relics of past encounters with his Rogue's Gallery — including an enormous, lifelike dinosaur, three-story tall coin, and dozens of confiscated weapons and gadgets — fill the cavernous space.

"It seems the city has begun to panic," Alfred, Bruce's loyal butler, says. He hands the Caped Crusader a cup of hot tea.

"Can you blame them, Alfred?" Bruce asks. "One minute it's hot enough to fry an egg on the cement. The next, that same cement is covered in snow."

Bruce turns on the computers, hoping to use them to pinpoint Mr. Freeze's location. The screens, many featuring maps of Gotham City, flicker and falter.

"It seems Freeze's dome has disrupted my satellite feed," Bruce says. "I'll have to rely on my detective skills to solve this mystery."

"It should be quite simple," Alfred says. "You've faced Victor Fries many times."

"His motive is always the same: to make others feel the kind of heartbreaking pain he did after losing his wife, Nora. And his icy inventions are often powered by diamonds." Bruce snaps his fingers. "I've got it!"

Turn the page.

Sitting on a small table nearby is a platter with the teapot and a plate of food. Rolled up next to them is the newest issue of the *Gotham Gazette.*

Bruce unrolls the newspaper and finds an article on the front page. ARCHEOLOGIST MAKES AMAZING DISCOVERY! reads the headline.

Bruce shows the paper to Alfred. "Dr. Arvin Schimmell, the world-famous archeologist, recently found a sealed pharaoh's tomb full of priceless gems. Gold, rubies, and one very large . . ."

"Diamond." Alfred easily finishes Bruce's sentence.

"Precisely," says Bruce. "The dig was funded by Wayne Enterprises, and the jewels are part of a new exhibit at the Gotham City Museum of Natural History."

Alfred smirks and says, "I'll fetch you a dry suit, sir."

***

One warm, dry Batsuit later, the Caped Crusader is back in action. The streets of Gotham City are covered in snow. Howling wind blows the powder into high drifts.

The city appears to be empty. Not a single soul is in sight. The Dark Knight is glad for this fact. He knows if things get messy with Mr. Freeze, there will be less chance of innocent people getting hurt.

The museum's main entrance is covered in a thick layer of ice. Icicles hang from the eaves. Frost creeps onto the edges of the museum's many windows. The whole building looks like an eerie ice palace.

Freeze must know I'm on to him, Batman thinks. *He's likely posted guards at every entrance. I've lost the element of surprise.*

The Dark Knight looks up and sees the museum's skylight high above. Though not impossible to reach, the subzero weather could make an aerial entrance more difficult.

Turn the page.

There are also tunnels beneath the streets that lead into the museum.

Perhaps Mr. Freeze does not know about them.

If Batman uses the tunnels, turn to page 73.
If Batman uses the skylight, turn to page 92.

The storeroom is a long, cavernous warehouse at the rear of the museum. It holds the remainder of the museum's priceless artifacts. There are rows and rows stacked high with crates. Scattered floodlights hang from the ceiling, giving off pockets of light. The remainder of the massive room is draped in blackness.

As Batman enters the storeroom, he hears the echoing voice of Mr. Freeze.

"Aha! It does exist, after all," the villain says. This is followed by the crack of splitting wood and a series of robotic whirring noises.

Batman follows the electronic sounds, clinging to the shadows.

He is very close, can almost see the mad scientist, when Mr. Freeze says, "My sweet Nora, what has become of you?"

Batman tenses. *Nora?*

Long ago, Nora Fries was Victor's wife. Her illness led to his transformation from scientist to super-villain.

Turn the page.

What does Freeze mean?

Batman rounds a corner and spies Mr. Freeze and a handful of henchmen nearby. A crate labeled ARKHAM EXHIBIT — part of the museum's collection of items taken from the infamous asylum — has been broken open. Inside must have been another of Freeze's robotic suits.

In the super-villain's hand, held up so that the light glints off its glass dome, is a snow globe with a pirouetting ballerina inside.

The snow globe's glass casing is cracked, and it looks to have been pieced back together and glued. Once, when Mr. Freeze was an inmate at Arkham Asylum, the globe was the last reminder of his lost wife. It was broken and lost during an escape.

Turn to page 50.

"Get the others and bring back the device," he orders the henchmen. "We're leaving."

"Yes, boss." The henchmen quickly dash back toward the Egyptian exhibit.

Straight toward Batman.

The Caped Crusader can hide in the shadowy storeroom aisles, between the crates, or leap atop the nearest crate. He must decide. There isn't a second to lose!

If Batman leaps atop the crates, turn to page 34.
If Batman hides between the crates, turn to page 88.

There is no time to lose.

Batman removes a small explosive device from his Utility Belt and attaches it to the slab of ice by the steps. He rushes to the far side of the hold, shields himself, and triggers the bomb.

BOOM!

Ice cracks and splinters all around him. Through the smoke, the Caped Crusader sees a thin crevice in the ice block where the bomb had exploded.

The steps, and safety, can be seen behind it through the haze.

Batman squeezes through the small opening left by the bomb. He can hear the ice still crackling as he makes his escape.

When the Dark Knight reaches the top of the steps and leaps back to the relative safety of the docks, he hears a police officer shout, "There's three of them! And they're getting away!"

The snow is coming down hard. The flakes are thick and wet.

Turn the page.

Batman quickly runs toward the warehouse, where Gordon and his officers stand with weapons drawn.

"Three of Victor Fries's henchmen were holed up in the warehouse," the commissioner tells Batman. "They've blasted two of my men with freeze guns."

"They're escaping!" another officer shouts.

The snow makes it hard to see. In the distance, Batman hears the squealing sounds of a truck driving away.

"I'll take it from here, Commissioner," the Dark Knight says.

Batman clicks a button on his Utility Belt, and the Batmobile roars to life. The roof slides open, and in one swift leap, the Dark Knight hops in. The roof closes after him.

VROOOM!

Batman stomps on the accelerator and swerves around the warehouse. The high-tech vehicle grips the icy streets.

Ahead in the driving snow, he spies an ice cream truck.

He follows it into the streets of Gotham City.

Turn to page 21.

The next chunk of ice from the bazooka could shatter the Batmobile's windshield. Or worse. At the next intersection, as the truck careens straight through, Batman makes a hard right turn.

He presses a button on the dashboard, and an overhead map of Gotham City flickers to life.

Then it falters. *The dome must be disrupting my satellite feed,* Batman concludes.

He tries to contact Alfred through his cowl. No luck.

Continuing on a parallel side street, Batman considers the most likely destination for the henchmen. And then it clicks into place.

Just blocks away is the Gotham Museum of Natural History.

Recently, a world-famous archeologist named Dr. Arvin Schimmell discovered a lost pharaoh's tomb. Inside the tomb were dozens of treasures, including gold statues, rubies and emeralds, and one enormous . . .

"Diamond," Batman says.

The large diamond was the crown jewel of Dr. Schimmell's expedition. Wayne Enterprises — run by Batman's alter ego, businessman Bruce Wayne — financed the dig. The Gotham Museum of Natural History is building an entire exhibit around it.

The Batmobile blasts through a snowdrift and back onto the henchmen's trail. Sure enough, the ice cream truck heads directly for the museum. It drives across the snow-covered lawn and crashes up the steps, into the building's main entrance.

The henchmen have not yet seen the Batmobile. Batman kills the car's lights and engine. He watches as Mr. Freeze's goons leap from the truck.

"Quick! Seal the door!" one shouts. The others use their ice guns to create a wall of ice around the building's entrance.

Mr. Freeze now knows I'm on to him, Batman thinks. *He'll post guards at every entrance. I've lost the element of surprise.*

Turn the page.

The Dark Knight looks up and sees the museum's skylight high above. Though not impossible to reach, the subzero weather could make an aerial entrance more difficult.

There are also tunnels beneath the streets that lead into the museum. Maybe Mr. Freeze doesn't know about them.

If Batman uses the tunnels, turn to page 14.
If Batman uses the skylight, turn to page 92.

Mr. Freeze turns to face the Dark Knight, sees the Batarang in his hands, and shouts, "No!"

Batman throws the weapon at the device. If he hits the diamond just right, and can knock it free, perhaps the dome around Gotham City will disappear.

However, the Batarang deflects off an invisible force field surrounding the device and clatters harmlessly to the floor.

Mr. Freeze laughs. "You fool," he says. Then he turns his freeze gun on Batman. Before the hero can move away, he is struck in the chest by a frozen blast.

"I'm sorry, Batman," Mr. Freeze says. "You will not save the day this time."

Then, Mr. Freeze's henchmen gather the device.

Frozen and helpless, Batman watches them escape.

THE END

To follow another path, turn to page 12.

Batman is uncertain where Mr. Freeze has gone, but a logical place to look is the museum's Arctic exhibit.

When he reaches the large hall, though, it is quiet. The middle of the room features a circular display of a glacier. A pool of water surrounds it. Two lifelike stuffed polar bears are perched on the fake ice.

There is no sign of Mr. Freeze.

Batman is about to leave when he hears a low grumble from behind him. The rumbling sound increases until it is a loud roar.

The hairs on Batman's neck rise as the hero turns to see the two polar bears — the ones he thought were part of the exhibit — leaping toward him!

When Mr. Freeze lived in the Arctic, he took in two polar bears as pets. Their names are Notchka and Shaka. It seems the two protective animals have joined their master on his latest trip to Gotham City.

One of the bears swipes at Batman with its enormous paw. The Dark Knight narrowly avoids its attack. As he turns to flee, he sees the second bear blocking the exit.

He is trapped.

The first polar bear lunges and snaps its jaws. Batman rolls backward, striking the wall. He is pinned, with nowhere to go.

Both bears advance on him. In his Utility Belt, Batman has a projectile net large enough for the creatures. But is there anything else that may work?

If Batman searches his Utility Belt for another option, turn to page 17.

If Batman uses the projectile net, turn to page 24.

Batman's hand reaches out, and he grips the handle of the item closest to him: the Joker's mallet. He lifts it high, and is about to swing it at Mr. Freeze, when his ears are filled with a loud hissing sound.

The mallet is emitting a green and purple gas, and it's spraying right at Batman!

Knockout gas, Batman thinks. *Just another of the Joker's many tricks . . .*

He's asleep before he finishes his thought.

Turn to page 62.

When Batman's eyes flutter open, he is staring at the storeroom ceiling. His instincts kick in immediately, and he leaps to his feet.

Mr. Freeze is nowhere to be seen.

At the far end of the storeroom, though, is a large metal door. Delivery trucks carrying art and artifacts use it to drop off their priceless cargo. The door is open, and swirling snow breezes into the storeroom.

Freeze must have just escaped, Batman thinks.

He dashes for the open door, hoping that Mr. Freeze has not gotten far.

As Batman reaches the delivery door, he hears the roar of many engines outside in the blizzard. Mr. Freeze and his goons are driving away on what appear to be snowmobiles. The super-villain's two pet polar bears, Notchka and Shaka, run beside Freeze, who is driving the lead machine.

Batman's hand goes to his Utility Belt.

The Batmobile is parked nearby and could easily intercept the fleeing Freeze. But the rear henchman — who revs his engine and begins to skitter across the snowfall — is close, too.

If Batman follows in the Batmobile, turn to page 66.
If Batman tries to steal the snowmobile, turn to page 82.

It is a long shot, but Batman's deductions are rarely wrong. He quickly types *GLOBE* into the keypad.

The device's hum grows louder, more intense. Batman must cup his hands over his ears to block out the noise.

Something is wrong.

A blue light emanates from the device. It pulses once with a blinding light.

Batman is thrown back onto the cement, knocked unconscious.

He wakes to find Commissioner Gordon staring down at him.

"Batman, are you all right?" the commissioner asks.

Batman looks around. Sunlight floods the streets of Gotham. The snow is melting. It drips from buildings and runs into the streets, making a slushy mess.

"Freeze's dome is gone," Batman says weakly. "It worked."

"I wish it were that simple," Gordon says. "Freeze is the one who spared us from the icy globe. Right before he fled Gotham City with the device and the Schimmell diamond."

If only the Dark Knight had tried one of the other possible passwords.

THE END

To follow another path, turn to page 12.

Clicking the button on his Utility Belt, Batman waits as the Batmobile squeals around the museum to his location. Its presence alerts the henchmen at the rear of Freeze's party.

"He's awake! Batman's after us, boss!" the henchman shouts.

Mr. Freeze turns his head, sees the Caped Crusader, and twists the throttle. His snowmobile disappears into the falling snow.

There's no time to lose. Batman leaps into the Batmobile and stomps on the accelerator. It races off in hot pursuit of the escaping super-villain.

The Batmobile roars through the snow-packed streets of Gotham City. Heavy flakes strike the windshield, making visibility nearly impossible. Batman passes a number of Freeze's henchmen on their snowmobiles. Some take aim at the car with their freeze guns, but their blue blasts miss hitting the sleek vehicle.

Ahead, Freeze makes a tight left turn, heading toward the bridge over the Gotham River. Batman follows . . .

. . . and must immediately slam on the brakes.

A semi-truck, abandoned by its driver, sits in the Batmobile's way. There is no way around the truck, making it impossible to cross the bridge.

Batman can only watch as Mr. Freeze and his henchmen speed away, enveloped by the falling snow.

THE END

To follow another path, turn to page 12.

Mr. Freeze turns to face the Dark Knight, sees the Batarang in his hands, and shouts, "No!"

Batman throws the weapon at Mr. Freeze, striking the villain at the base of his helmet. Sparks and streams of cold gas immediately begin to spray from Mr. Freeze's suit.

"Arrghh!" The super-villain's arms drop to his sides.

"Finish him!" shouts Mr. Freeze, disappearing down a darkened hallway.

"You heard him!" one henchman shouts. "Get Batman!"

The Dark Knight readies himself for action. Mr. Freeze's goons surround him on all sides. He counts eight of them. They are all armed with freeze guns.

Eager to fulfill their boss's wish, all eight of the henchmen fire at once.

Turn to page 70.

It will take all his skill to avoid becoming a bat-shaped ice sculpture.

Batman's instincts and martial arts training kick in. He twists and turns, evading the bluish blasts of ice.

The Dark Knight leaps into the air, unfurling his cape and spinning like a twisting tornado. The cape's ultra-strong fabric deflects the icy beams, sending them in all directions. When the super hero finally lands, his cape is momentarily frozen stiff.

BWEEOOM! BWEEOOM!

The henchman continue to blast.

The sunny, sand-colored Egyptian exhibit hall turns into a winter wonderland. Icicles dangle from the Sphinx's chin. The sarcophagus is turned into an ice cube.

The frustrated henchmen's aim grows erratic. Batman barely dodges an errant beam, slamming into the side of a pyramid.

"Oof!" The air explodes from Batman's lungs.

The Caped Crusader has had enough. He snatches a capsule from his Utility Belt and drops it to the floor.

PFFFFTTT!

Suddenly, the hall is filled with a hazy fog. The henchmen begin to cough and choke. Batman places his rebreather into his mouth, allowing him to breathe in fresh oxygen.

Ducking low, the Dark Knight then scrambles through the haze. Around him, the henchmen have stopped firing. They continue to cough and bump around in confusion.

"Hey! I caught him!" one henchman shouts.

"That's me, you fool!" another grumbles.

Batman sees the device and the Schimmell diamond. He reaches in to grab the gem —

— and his hand is instantly repelled.

It has a force field of its own, Batman thinks. *There must be a way to turn it off. I have to find Mr. Freeze.*

Turn the page.

Batman heads off into the darkened hall.

The hall splits in two directions. One leads to the museum's storeroom, the other to the Arctic exhibit. But which way did the super-villain go?

If Batman heads to the storeroom, turn to page 47.
If Batman heads to the Arctic exhibit, turn to page 58.

Batman knows Gotham City's underground labyrinth well. There is a sewer entrance nearby that leads directly into the museum, near the boiler room.

The Dark Knight climbs down into the sewers. There is heat left trapped beneath the city, and the tunnels are warm. Batman runs through them, using the night-vision goggles in his cowl to see. Rats squeak and scurry out of his way.

Sure enough, the tunnels lead him directly under the museum's boiler room. He climbs a ladder leading to the floor grate.

The grate, however, is covered in ice.

Before he can pry it free, Batman uses his small torch to thaw the ice around the metal.

The boiler room is coated from floor to ceiling with icicles and frost. The boiler, a hulking metal machine in the middle of the room, is cold and dark.

Freeze has cut the heat to the whole building, Batman thinks.

Turn the page.

There is no one lurking outside in the basement hall. Batman sticks to the shadows, running silently to the nearest stairwell.

He knows precisely where to find Mr. Freeze. The villain — and Dr. Schimmell's breathtaking diamond — will most certainly be in the museum's Ancient Egypt exhibit.

Turn to page 27.

As he chases after Mr. Freeze, Batman keeps a safe distance. He maneuvers around abandoned cars and trucks while the super-villain rides along the walking path on the edge of the bridge.

On the other side, Batman gains ground again, until his snowmobile is inches away from Mr. Freeze.

"There's nowhere to go, Freeze!" Batman shouts.

The super-villain turns. In his hand is his freeze gun.

Batman lets up on the throttle, falling back as Mr. Freeze fires. The blast narrowly misses the snowmobile. Instead, it paints the snowy ground in front of the vehicle with ice.

When the twin treads of his snowmobile hit the slick patch, Batman feels the vehicle begin to spin out.

He's going to crash!

As the snowmobile begins to spin out, Batman leaps from the seat.

Turn the page.

The super hero goes flying through the air, hits the snow-packed street, and tumbles safely. Ahead, Mr. Freeze turns, preparing to finish off the Caped Crusader, who stands in the street, exposed, nowhere to go.

Mr. Freeze aims the ice gun . . . and does not see the hood of a buried car, lost in a snowdrift in the street.

The snowmobile flips, and Mr. Freeze goes flying through the air. The globe device detaches from his back and lands in the snowy street next to the villain.

Batman runs to his fallen foe.

Lying on the cement beside him is the shattered snow globe. Its porcelain ballerina is broken in half.

"No," Mr. Freeze wails. Despite his emotionless nature, there is pain in his voice. "I cannot lose you again, my love."

Batman crouches beside Mr. Freeze and grabs a remote control keypad from the villain's hand.

"What's the password, Victor?" Batman asks. "How do I shut off the device?"

"I'll never tell you," Freeze responds.

Batman quickly deduces the three likeliest possibilities: Globe, Nora, and Fries. But which one could it possibly be?

If Batman enters the password "FRIES," turn to page 32.

If Batman enters the password "GLOBE," turn to page 64.

If Batman enters the password "NORA," turn to page 103.

Batman's hand wraps around the handle of the Penguin's umbrella. He does not know what to expect; Oswald Cobblepot's parasols are unpredictable at best. The Caped Crusader holds the umbrella toward Mr. Freeze and flips the trigger in the handle.

A strong white bolt of electricity zaps from the umbrella's tip. It strikes Mr. Freeze in the chest.

"My suit!" Freeze claws at his suit as it crackles and sparks. Fingers of energy wrap around the villain. The suit short-circuits, and Freeze topples to the cement floor.

As he falls, Mr. Freeze bumps the crate on which the snow globe is resting. Batman catches it before it shatters on the cement.

"You can't win, Freeze," Batman says to the immobile villain.

"Oh no!" From the entrance of the storeroom come the gasps of numerous henchmen.

Batman turns to see Freeze's men.

Two of the henchmen, wearing thick gloves, are carrying the device with the diamond perched on top.

They must have turned off the force field surrounding it, Batman thinks.

Mr. Freeze's goons drop the device with a crash, and it clatters to the storeroom's cement floor. They turn and make a run for it.

Batman ignores the fleeing henchmen. He turns to Freeze and says, "What's the password, Victor?"

"Because you saved my love," Freeze says, referring to the snow globe, "I will tell you how to stop this eternal winter."

When the password escapes his lips, Batman thinks, *Of course. There's really nothing else it could be, is there?* He types the letters into the villain's remote control keypad, and immediately there is a change in the air.

Batman runs toward a large delivery door leading outside. He throws it open.

Turn the page.

The snow has stopped falling. The wind has stopped howling. He looks to the sky.

The icy globe trapping the city has vanished.

"Great work, Batman," Commissioner Gordon says.

An hour has passed since the icy globe over Gotham City was turned off. Police officers swarm the storeroom. Mr. Freeze stands nearby, wearing an elaborate set of restraints.

"The diamond and device are safe," Gordon continues. "We rounded up Freeze's men, as well as two . . . uh, polar bears."

Batman watches two nervous animal control department officials lead Notchka and Shaka to a waiting truck.

"Freeze can cool his heels at Arkham now," Batman says. "Here." He hands the commissioner the snow globe. "Make sure he gets this."

A puzzled Gordon takes the globe.

"By the way, what's today's forecast?" Batman asks with a smirk.

"Looks like it's gonna be a hot one," Gordon answers. "Thankfully."

THE END

To follow another path, turn to page 12.

Before the last henchman can get away, Batman fires his grapnel gun. The hook catches the back of the goon's puffy winter coat. With a yank, Batman pulls the man from his snowmobile. The vehicle slows, then putters to a stop.

"Thanks for letting me borrow your ride," Batman says as he passes the dazed henchman, who lies almost buried in a pile of snow. He leaps onto the snowmobile, guns the engine, and rockets after the escaping Mr. Freeze.

It has only been a few hours since the icy globe fell over Gotham City, but already, the snowfall measures over a foot. High drifts block doorways. Cars parked along the street are buried and hard to see.

Batman weaves past the remaining henchmen on their snowmobiles. One tries to fire an icy blast at him, but the Caped Crusader ducks and the beam harmlessly strikes a street sign.

Mr. Freeze glances back and sees Batman hot on his tail.

"Notchka! Shaka! Attack!"

The polar bears stop and turn to face the oncoming hero. As they rear up on their hind legs, Batman spies a snowdrift to his left. He hits it perfectly, soaring high in the air, right over the two menacing polar bears!

Turn to page 85.

The Caped Crusader's airborne snowmobile lands safely back on the road. It swerves left and right, but Batman regains control.

Mr. Freeze is the only one left to catch.

Batman spies the dome's device — and the Schimmell diamond — strapped to the super-villain's back. He guns the throttle and pushes the snowmobile to its limits.

Mr. Freeze makes a tight left turn, driving onto a metal bridge. Below it flows the Gotham River. Batman follows.

Cars and trucks sit abandoned in the middle of the bridge. Mr. Freeze must slow down to weave around them. Batman pulls in close. If he times it right, he should be able to leap aboard Freeze's snowmobile.

If Batman stays on his own snowmobile, turn to page 75.
If Batman leaps onto Freeze's snowmobile, turn to page 96.

With lightning-quick reflexes, Batman draws his grapnel gun and shoots it at the ceiling. Its hook catches on a steel girder, and the Dark Knight is lifted into the sky just as the henchman unleashes a blue beam of ice.

However, the frosty blast strikes Batman's fluttering cape, sending the hero off-course. He swings into the large, ice-covered Tyrannosaurus rex skeleton, hitting it solidly with his shoulder. Batman loses his grip on the grapnel gun, and he falls back to the museum's marble floor.

Batman lands hard on his back, and the air is forced from his lungs. Above him, he hears the cracking of frozen bones, as the dinosaur skeleton sways back and forth.

"Look out!" one of Mr. Freeze's goons says to the other. "It's gonna fall!"

Sure enough, Batman watches as the Tyrannosaurus rex's skeleton splits apart like a tumbling jigsaw puzzle. He does not have time to move. He can only shield himself with his cape and hope he is not hit.

Bones crash to the floor all around him. The beast's ribcage smashes down atop him, trapping the Dark Knight within like a prison cell.

Batman tries to lift the avalanche of bones but cannot.

He is trapped!

THE END

To follow another path, turn to page 12.

There may not be time to leap atop the crates, so the Dark Knight simply slips between two rows of them. He cloaks himself in shadow alongside a collection of ancient statues. For years, Batman has trained his body to be still and silent. He breathes long and slow through his nostrils.

What he does not expect is for several of Mr. Freeze's men to split from the others and take an alternate route out of the storeroom.

They run through the aisle where Batman stands, coming within inches of colliding with the super hero.

The last man trips on Batman's black boot.

"Hey!" the guy grumbles. He looks up, right into the sneer of the Caped Crusader. "What the —?"

Batman has been discovered!

Batman quickly wraps his cape around the henchman and covers his mouth with one hand. It's too late, though. Others have seen him.

"Boss!" one of the henchmen shouts. His voice echoes in the storeroom. "Batman's here!"

The henchmen attack, and Batman does a valiant job of fending them off.

A strong thug drives his shoulder into a Mayan statue, a tall stone carving of the bat-like creature that guards the underworld. The statue wobbles, then crashes down . . .

. . . right onto Batman!

As Batman tries to free himself, Mr. Freeze strides over, freeze gun in hand. He shakes his head in its robotic helmet. "You fool," he says.

Before Batman can say anything, he's encased in a block of ice, doomed to watch Mr. Freeze escape into the wintery city.

THE END

To follow another path, turn to page 12.

The snow is coming down strong, and Batman is afraid if he steers away from the ice cream truck, he will lose the henchmen's trail for good.

Maybe I can stop them by taking out their tire with a well-placed missile, he thinks.

Batman flicks on the Batmobile's targeting device, carefully aiming at one of the truck's rear tires.

The temporary distraction has taken Batman's eyes from the road in front of him. He doesn't notice the ice chunk fired from the henchmen's bazooka until it is too late. What was once a small, spider-web crack in the Batmobile's windshield turns into an explosion of shattered glass.

Batman instinctively raises a hand to protect himself. The wind and cold come howling in, and the Dark Knight loses control of his vehicle.

It slams into a snowdrift, burying the hood in powder. Batman tries to disengage the roof, but it is stuck.

The henchmen stop their truck. One of them jumps out. Through the wind, Batman hears him shout, "Tell Mr. Freeze we just put Batman on ice."

He aims a freeze gun at the Batmobile, and before the Dark Knight can do anything, the henchman covers the whole vehicle in an enormous glacier.

Batman is trapped in his cool confines until Mr. Freeze shuts off the dome or the police arrive and free him.

THE END

To follow another path, turn to page 12.

"I'm Batman, not a rat," the Caped Crusader says under his breath. He removes the grapnel gun from his waist, slinks to the museum's wall, and fires into the air.

The hook wraps around a pipe. Batman attaches the gun to his belt and is whisked into the sky by an ultra-strong wire.

He lands light as a feather on his feet atop the building. The skylight is near. He carefully crosses the snow-covered roof, crouching down to glance through the window and into the museum.

Below is the darkened Prehistoric exhibit hall. Large skeletons of a Tyrannosaurus rex, a Stegosaurus, and others fill the hall.

Two of Mr. Freeze's henchmen are guarding the exhibit.

Turn to page 94.

Batman crashes through the skylight, cape spread wide. Shattered glass rains down on the unsuspecting henchmen. The Dark Knight lands on his feet in the shadows of the enormous T. rex skeleton.

"It's Batman!" one of the goons shouts. "Quick! Tell the boss!"

As the second henchman snatches the walkie-talkie from his belt, Batman throws a Batarang. Sparks fly as it connects with the communication device.

The first thug aims his freeze gun at Batman and fires.

ZAP!

The Caped Crusader dives aside. He throws a second Batarang — this one equipped with a rope — and expertly ties up the henchman's legs. Batman pulls the rope, and the thug falls hard onto his back. The freeze gun flies from his hand. It blasts upward, coating the T. rex skeleton with an icy sheen.

ZAP!

A blue blast from the second henchman whizzes past Batman's shoulder. The Dark Knight dives aside, out into the middle of the hall, exposed. The first thug's fallen freeze gun lies near his feet.

The remaining henchman trains his weapon. His next shot is sure to stop Batman in his tracks.

If Batman goes for the freeze gun on the floor, turn to page 26.

If Batman uses his grapnel gun to escape, turn to page 86.

The snowmobiles are inches apart. If Batman is going to act, the time is now.

He leaps from his own vehicle and lands perfectly on the back of Freeze's snowmobile.

"You fool! What are you doing?" an angered Mr. Freeze shouts. Batman's added weight makes the snowmobile swerve back and forth.

They are racing along the bridge's walking path, near the edge.

Batman grapples with the villain's glass helmet. Mr. Freeze drives an elbow back into the Caped Crusader's stomach, knocking the air from his lungs. Freeze turns and aims his ice gun at Batman.

The snowmobile loses traction and hits a snowdrift. Before either passenger can react, they crash over the side of the bridge and out into thin air!

Batman, Mr. Freeze, and the snowmobile plummet toward the dark waters of the Gotham River.

Though the river is not frozen yet, large chunks of ice float downstream.

Batman reaches out and grabs his cape with both hands. He spreads it wide, slowing his fall and gliding safely to the river's bank. Mr. Freeze cannot do the same, and he splashes into the cold water.

Batman waits for a long time for the super-villain to surface. He does not. However, the air suddenly ripples and the driving snow thins and clears. Batman looks up into the sky. The icy globe surrounding Gotham glows a faint blue before disappearing entirely.

The cold depths of the Gotham River have saved the city.

***

Hours later, Batman watches from above on the bridge as police divers work in the river. Daybreak has filled the city once more with light, and though it is still morning, it is already quite warm. Soon, the blazing heat will melt away all of the snow.

Turn the page.

Now, it is just a slushy, sloppy mess.

Standing beside the Caped Crusader is Commissioner Gordon.

"I know it doesn't feel like a victory," Gordon says, "but thank you, Batman. Gotham City owes you another one."

"Mr. Freeze has escaped," the Dark Knight replies.

"At least he no longer has the ability to create his icy globe," Gordon says, pointing to another pair of divers as they remove the metallic device from the water.

Batman notices an empty space at the top of the contraption. "Where is Dr. Schimmell's diamond?" he asks, though he already knows the answer.

Gordon's men spend most of the day searching for the large gem, but they do not find it. Batman knows they'll never find it here. The super hero is certain that wherever Mr. Freeze has gone, he has taken the diamond with him.

The Caped Crusader has thwarted Mr. Freeze's plans, but he fears he will not be so lucky the next time the cold-hearted villain appears in Gotham City.

THE END

To follow another path, turn to page 12.

Batman instinctively reaches for his grapnel gun. He fires the weapon at the escaping truck.

BLAM! The hook locks onto one of the back door's handles.

As the wire goes taut, Batman is pulled forward. Like a water-skier, the Caped Crusader slides on both feet over the snow-covered street. He retracts the grapnel gun, which draws him close to the truck. In one swift leap, Batman is atop the fleeing vehicle.

A hatch at the top of the truck pops open, and one of the henchmen pokes his head out. Batman delivers an uppercut to the goon's jaw, dazing him.

He falls back into the truck.

Batman follows.

The ice cream truck is cramped inside, and the first thing Batman sees is a freeze gun pointed right at him.

He ducks low as a blue beam blasts past him. It hits the truck's windshield, turning it to frost.

"Hey!" shouts the driver. He wipes at the frost, trying to see outside.

Another one of the henchmen holds a cylinder in his hand. There is a pin on the side.

"Don't use that!" another shouts. "That's a Freeze Pop. It'll turn this whole truck to —"

The ice cream truck suddenly lurches to the side.

"We're gonna crash!" shouts the frightened truck driver.

Batman looks for something to hold onto as the truck topples onto its side. ***WHAM!***

The Caped Crusader feels like he's in a clothes dryer as he and Mr. Freeze's henchmen flail about.

"Oh no!" the henchman holding the cylinder cries out.

Batman looks over to see the Freeze Pop has fallen from the goon's hand. As it hits the truck's side door — which is now below them — it explodes in a brilliant blue light.

Turn the page.

When Batman can see again, he discovers that he cannot move. The entire inside of the toppled truck is coated in ice. He and the henchmen are frozen in place.

There's no way he'll be able to free himself in time to stop Mr. Freeze.

THE END

To follow another path, turn to page 12.

There is only one logical, almost predictable password. Victor Fries may have a cold heart, but he was once filled with love. And perhaps there's a bit of humanity left in the man.

Batman types the name *NORA* into the keypad.

Immediately, the humming sound emitted by the device wanes, then stops. The air ripples and the driving snow thins and clears. Batman looks up into the sky. The icy globe surrounding Gotham glows a faint blue before disappearing entirely.

"Great work, Batman."

Commissioner Gordon and a number of Gotham police officers swarm the slushy street. The snow is melting, making the clean-up sloppy work. Mr. Freeze, now wearing an elaborate set of restraints, is being helped into an armored police truck.

Turn to page 105.

"Victor Fries can cool his heels at Arkham for a while," Batman says.

"We've rounded up the last of Freeze's men," Gordon says, "as well as . . . uh, two polar bears."

Nearby, a handful of scientists examine Mr. Freeze's device. One is gingerly removing the Schimmell diamond.

The sun rises over Gotham, casting the skyline in beautiful, bright light. A new day has begun.

"What's today's weather forecast?" Batman asks with a smirk.

"Looks like it's gonna be a hot one," Gordon answers. "Thankfully."

THE END

To follow another path, turn to page 12.

AUTHOR

Brandon Terrell is the author of numerous children's books, including six volumes in the Tony Hawk's 900 Revolution series and several Sports Illustrated Kids Graphic Novels. When not hunched over his laptop writing, Brandon enjoys watching movies, reading, baseball, and spending time with his wife and two children in Minnesota.

ILLUSTRATOR

Ethen Beaver is a professional comic book artist from Modesto, California. His best-known works for DC Comics include Justice League Unlimited and Legion of Superheroes in the 31st Century. He has also illustrated for other top publishers, including Marvel, Dark Horse, and Abrams.

GLOSSARY

ambushed (AM-bushd)—hid and then attacked someone

artifacts (ART-uh-fakts)—objects made or changed by human beings, especially a tool or weapon used in the past

asylum (uh-SYE-lum)—a hospital for people who are mentally ill and cannot live by themselves

glacier (GLAY-shur)—a huge sheet of ice found in mountain valleys or polar regions

labyrinth (LAH-buh-rinth)—a garden maze formed by paths separated by high hedges

navigates (NAV-uh-gates)—makes one's way over or through

projectile (pruh-JEK-tuhl)—an object, such as a bullet or missile, that is thrown or shot through the air

sarcophagus (sar-KAH-fah-guhss)—a stone coffin

Sphinx (SFINGKS)—a large statue found in Giza, Egypt, of a creature with the body of a lion and the head of a woman, ram, or hawk

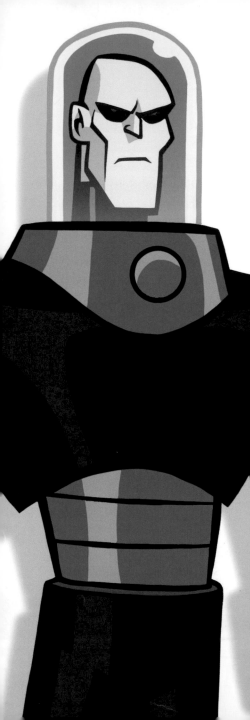

MR. FREEZE

Real Name:
Dr. Victor Fries

Occupation:
Professional Criminal,
Scientist

Base:
Gotham City

Height:
6 feet

Weight:
190 lbs.

Eyes:
Icy blue

Hair:
None

Victor Fries felt lonely throughout his schooling. He was teased constantly by classmates and was sure he'd never have a friend. Then he met Nora, and everything changed. They fell in love. But when Nora became ill with an incurable disease, Victor lost hope. To say Mr. Freeze's heart went cold would be an understatement. His indifference toward human life is now so severe that he spreads suffering to anyone within his icy grasp. That way, other people will feel his pain.

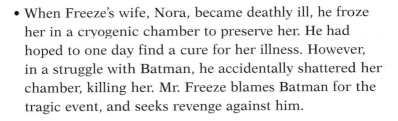

- When Freeze's wife, Nora, became deathly ill, he froze her in a cryogenic chamber to preserve her. He had hoped to one day find a cure for her illness. However, in a struggle with Batman, he accidentally shattered her chamber, killing her. Mr. Freeze blames Batman for the tragic event, and seeks revenge against him.

- After being exposed to various chemicals, Mr. Freeze's body composition was forever changed. He requires constant refrigeration, or his lungs will melt and his blood will boil.

- Mr. Freeze has the tools to match his icy schemes. He uses a freeze weapon that turns his enemies into blocks of ice. He also wears a cryogenic suit that chills him to the subzero temperature his body needs to survive. His suit also grants him strength and durability.

THE FUN DOESN'T STOP HERE!
DISCOVER MORE AT...
WWW.CAPSTONEKIDS.COM
FIND COOL WEBSITES AND MORE BOOKS LIKE THIS ONE AT WWW.FACTHOUND.COM.
JUST TYPE IN THE BOOK ID: 9781434297082 AND YOU'RE READY TO GO!